BABY
BAND

Diane Jackson Hill

Illustrated by Giuseppe Poli

NEW FRONTIER PUBLISHING

The apartment block loomed cold and quiet.
The same people had lived there a long time.

They did not know each other and they
never spoke – not even to say hello.

But then THE BABY arrived.
The baby cried.
The baby cried a lot.

The baby could be heard in
every room of apartment 8A.

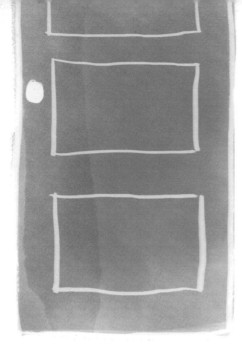

The baby could be heard in every apartment on level 8.

His mother tried everything.
She rocked his cot.
She cuddled him.

She gave him soft, fluffy toys and read him stories.
The baby cried and cried until one day …

he found some pots and pans.
The baby held a shiny lid in one hand and
a chunky pot in the other. Then he crashed
them together as hard as he could –

CLANG.
'AHHH!'
screamed his mother in fright.

The baby laughed. He did it again.
And again.
And again.

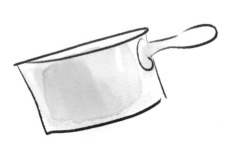

His mother screamed again and again and again, just for fun.

CLANG. 'AHHH!'

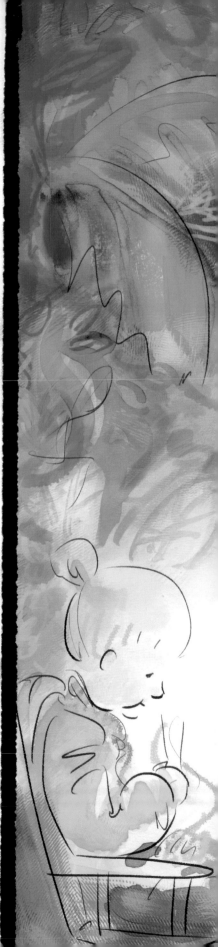

The grandma in 8B sprang out of her rocking chair
every time she heard the scream.

CLANG AHHH
SQUEAK, SQUAWK

The teenager in 8C thought this
sounded cool. He added a stomp.

CLANG AHHH SQUEAK, SQUAWK STOMP

The sisters in 8D were grating carrot. They joined in.

CLANG AHHH SQUEAK, SQUAWK STOMP CHA-CHA-CHA

The teacher in 8E always sang when he washed the dishes. He added a note or two.

CLANG AHHH SQUEAK, SQUAWK STOMP CHA-CHA-CHA DOO WAH

The window cleaner working in 8F listened, but
did not add anything.
'It's good to leave a space,' he thought.

Everybody was having so much fun,
they flung open their doors.

CLANG AHHH
SQUEAK, SQUAWK

STOMP CHA-CHA-CHA DOO WAH ... WHOMP

Way down the passage they shimmied and they shuffled.

And onto the rooftop they hooted and they hustled.

But where was that baby?
He had not made a peep.

He was snug inside the big bass drum.

Fast asleep.

To my mum, Melba, who gifted me the
love of music-making. DJH

To Oscar, Georgette and Darcy,
for each clang, bang, stomp and ahhh!
I love them all. GP